Dear Parent:
Your child's love of r

Every child learns to read in a different way and at his or her own speed. Some go back and forth between reading levels and read favorite books again and again. Others read through each level in order. You can help your young reader improve and become more confident by encouraging his or her own interests and abilities. From books your child reads with you to the first books he or she reads alone, there are I Can Read Books for every stage of reading:

SHARED READING
Basic language, word repetition, and whimsical illustrations, ideal for sharing with your emergent reader

BEGINNING READING
Short sentences, familiar words, and simple concepts for children eager to read on their own

READING WITH HELP
Engaging stories, longer sentences, and language play for developing readers

READING ALONE
Complex plots, challenging vocabulary, and high-interest topics for the independent reader

ADVANCED READING
Short paragraphs, chapters, and exciting themes for the perfect bridge to chapter books

I Can Read Books have introduced children to the joy of reading since 1957. Featuring award-winning authors and illustrators and a fabulous cast of beloved characters, I Can Read Books set the standard for beginning readers.

A lifetime of discovery begins with the magical words "I Can Read!"

Visit www.icanread.com for information
on enriching your child's reading experience.

The Land Before Time: The Lonely Dinosaur © 2007 Universal Studios Licensing LLLP. The Land Before Time and related characters are trademarks and copyrights of Universal Studios and U-Drive Productions, Inc. Licensed by Universal Studios Licensing LLLP. All rights reserved. Printed in China. No part of this book may be used or reproduced in any manner whatsoever without written permission except in the case of brief quotations embodied in critical articles and reviews. For information address HarperCollins Children's Books, a division of HarperCollins Publishers, 10 East 53rd Street, New York, NY 10022.
www.icanread.com
Library of Congress Catalog card number: 2007926271
ISBN 978-0-06-135293-5
Typography by Rick Farley 11 12 13 14 SCP 10 9 8 7 6 5 4 3 2 ❖ First Edition

I Can Read!

READING 2 WITH HELP

THE LAND BEFORE TIME™

The Lonely Dinosaur

Adapted by Catherine Hapka
Illustrated by Charles Grosvenor
and Artful Doodlers
Screenplay by Noelle Wright

HarperCollins*Publishers*

Chomper: A friendly young Sharptooth.

Spike: A strong, silent Spiketail.

Ducky: A kind, loyal Swimmer.

Littlefoot: Chomper's smart Longneck friend.

Chomper covers Spike's eyes with mud.
"Now find Ducky using only
your sniffer," Chomper says.
Spike grunts. He sniffs the air and sets
off on this game of hide-and-seek.

Sniff, sniff!

Spike follows his nose.

He finds a weed and some brambles.

Then he smells something else.

Could it be Ducky?

Spike wipes the mud from his eyes.

It falls on a foot.

But it's not Ducky's foot.

It belongs to grumpy Mr. Threehorn.

Chomper covers Spike's eyes again.

"Keep trying, Spike," he says.

Sniff, sniff! Spike tries again.

This time he finds Ducky!

"Way to go, Spike!" Chomper cries.

Later, Chomper sees the grown-ups

setting out green food.

Today is the feast of

the Time of Great Giving.

"What's it all about?" Chomper asks.

"Our party is about sharing
and not having to worry
about Sharpteeth!" Tria tells him.

Chomper frowns.

He is a Sharptooth!

Chomper finds Littlefoot
and his grandpa picking tree stars.
"Sharpteeth used to keep us from
eating tree stars," Grandpa says.
"We had to eat swamp sticks!"

"Yuck!" Littlefoot cries.

Chomper feels confused.

He is the only Sharptooth

in the Great Valley.

He does not eat green food.

Does that make him too different?

Soon it is time for the feast.

There is nothing for Chomper to eat!

There is only green food.

Chomper wonders if he belongs

in the Great Valley after all.

"Maybe I should go back
to the Mysterious Beyond,"
he says to Ducky.
The Mysterious Beyond is where
all the other Sharpteeth live.

"No, no, no!" Ducky cries.

"You are a nice Sharptooth.

You taught Spike to use his sniffer.

You are a very good teacher,

Chomper!"

That gives Chomper an idea.

"Maybe I can teach other Sharpteeth

how to be nice, too!

Thanks for the idea, Ducky!"

After the feast,

everyone wonders where Chomper is.

"He said something about

teaching the Sharpteeth

how to be friends," Ducky says.

The others are worried.

"We'd better find him fast,"
Littlefoot says.

"We can sniff for him," Ducky says.

"Chomper showed Spike how!"

Sniff, sniff!

Spike does what Chomper taught him.

He leads the others into

the Mysterious Beyond. . . .

Meanwhile Chomper is looking

for other Sharpteeth.

He decides to rest in a cave.

Uh-oh!

Somebody is already in there!

Chomper sees three Sharpteeth.

"Maybe we can be friends," he says.

But they don't want to be friends.

They roar and chase him away.

Later Chomper sees more Sharpteeth.

They are running away from Red Claw.

"I'll never be able to teach him

to be nice!" Chomper tells himself.

Red Claw is very, very mean!

Finally Chomper finds

a Sharptooth his own age.

"Want to be friends?" Chomper asks.

He tries to teach

the young Sharptooth to play catch.

The Sharptooth tries to bite him!

"Ouch!" Chomper says.

"We bite our food, not our friends!"

Just then he hears a loud roar.

"Uh-oh," he says.

Two grown-up Sharpteeth see Chomper.

They are angry and they chase him.

He runs up a mountain to get away.

"So much for making friends!"

says Chomper.

He climbs up to an icy ledge where

the Sharpteeth can't follow him.

Suddenly he hears a loud crack.

The ledge breaks off

and Chomper slides down the hill!

Sniff, sniff.

Spike and the others

are still searching for Chomper.

Ruby hears a faraway yell.

"Sounds like Chomper!" she says.

Chomper's friends find him
in an icy gorge.

How can they get him out?

Spike knows!

He starts to eat the ice.

Soon Chomper can climb to safety.

"Let's get out of here!" he says.

The kids slide down the mountain

and hurry back to the Great Valley.

"You left the Time of Great Giving
before we gave you your feast,"
Littlefoot tells Chomper.
The others show Chomper a feast
of his favorite tasty bugs.

Now Chomper knows for sure
that he belongs with his friends
and not with the Sharpteeth.
"Yum. Thanks, everyone," he says.
"Anyone want to share?"